LET THE
LYNX
COME IN

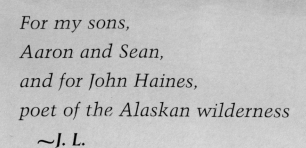

For my sons,
Aaron and Sean,
and for John Haines,
poet of the Alaskan wilderness
   ~J. L.

For Zoe
   ~P. B.

First published 1996 by Walker Books Ltd
87 Vauxhall Walk, London SE11 5HJ

This edition published 1998

10 9 8 7 6 5 4 3 2 1

Text © 1996 Jonathan London
Illustrations © 1996 Patrick Benson

This book has been typeset in Trump Mediaeval.

Printed in Singapore

British Library Cataloguing in Publication Data
A catalogue record for this book is
available from the British Library.

ISBN 0-7445-6041-1

LET THE
LYNX
COME IN

Written by
Jonathan London

Illustrated by
Patrick Benson

WALKER BOOKS
AND SUBSIDIARIES
LONDON • BOSTON • SYDNEY

As the fire snaps
and roars
in the pot-belly stove,
my father snores,
but I can't sleep.
It was his idea
to come
to the north woods
where I've never
been before.

There are wolves
and bears out there.
And a lynx.

I hear a scratching
coming from outside.
I get up, creep to the door,
open it a crack,
then jump back…

A WILDCAT!

The lynx steps in,
shakes first one paw
then the other;
stands still as a stone,
quiet as an owl,
in the middle of the room.
Firelight glows
in its yellow eyes.

I shiver
in the warm room
as the lynx grows
and grows
and grows,

till its whiskers
touch the walls!

Great Lynx commands
with his silence.
I grab fistfuls of fur
and climb up and up
on to the back
of the enormous cat.
And the next thing
I know ...

we're outside in the snow!

Bunched like a fist
I clench fur
as Great Lynx creeps
on big cat's feet.
If I cry, my tears
will turn to ice.

In the trees
the moon trembles
on a bare black branch,
then rolls along with us
through the hard
northern night.

Great Lynx leaps
across a frozen river,
steps across
glittering snow,
stalking some
invisible thing.
We climb a ridge of ice
and there it is!

Great Lynx stops
and crouches.
And together we watch
the dance
of the northern lights.

In an explosion of snow
Great Lynx leaps
into the sky!
I cling
to the wildcat's back
as we claw up and up
the curtains of light …

and land with a pounce
on the big round moon.
Suddenly
I'm filled with stars
and moonlight.
Great Lynx purrs
and if I could
I would purr too.

I yawn and drowsily say,
"Lynx, let's go home!"

Down and down
we ripple through the night,
down the curtains
of light ...
till we flop
like a pile of snow
before my cabin.

I climb off,
turn at the door.
Before my eyes
Great Lynx shrinks
down and down.
He crouches and
I feel his gaze inside me
like fire
from the northern lights.

He shakes a paw
and slowly bounds away
through the silent night.

The pot-belly's
still chugging.
My dad's still snoring.
I curl up
and gaze at the fire.

As I close my eyes
and sink into sleep,
I say …

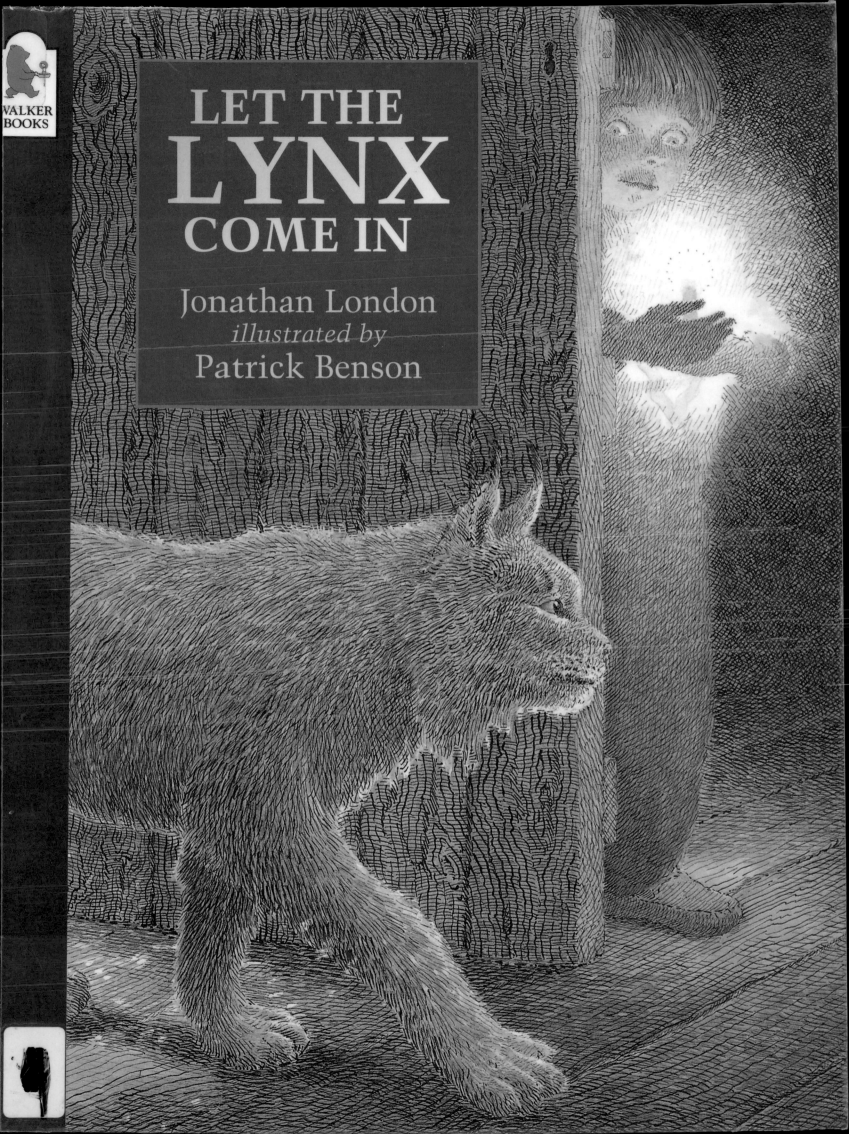

LET THE LYNX COME IN

Jonathan London

illustrated by

Patrick Benson

"Let the lynx come in."

And the lynx sleeps
curled in my dream
like the moon.